THE GIRL WITH SOMETHING EXTRA

By
DENZIL CASTO

A THOMAS THOMAS THRILLER
Based on a true event

Order this book online at www.trafford.com
or email orders@trafford.com

Most Trafford titles are also available at major online book retailers.

Printed in Victoria, BC, Canada.

ISBN: 978-1-4269-2353-1 (Soft)

Library of Congress Control Number: 2009913599

*Our mission is to efficiently provide the world's finest, most comprehensive
book publishing service, enabling every author to experience success.
To find out how to publish your book, your way, and have it available
worldwide, visit us online at www.trafford.com*

Trafford rev. 12/23/2009

 www.trafford.com

North America & international
toll-free: 1 888 232 4444 (USA & Canada)
phone: 250 383 6864 ♦ fax: 812 355 4082

The phone brought me out of a deep sleep. Her leg was slung over my body. The sheet covered her face. For a second or two I couldn't remember who it was. Her silver dollar size nipple was standing at attention due to the blast of the air conditioner. I grabbed the phone. Detective Thomas here ,"how may I help you?" Its was "Arkie" Detective Willard Everett, "theres been another one." Meet me 15th. Ave. and Monroe. See you 15 minutes or so. I went in the bathroom, did natures call, put some toothpaste on my tongue, swished it around in my mouth. Run my hand through my hair, Ok that's it for today.

I went back in the bedroom. She was stuffing her panties and bra in her jeans pocket. It was Bonnie Van Buren, Lt. Jerry Van Buren wife. She pulled a tee shirt over her head, kissed me on the cheek and left.

I grabbed a cold coke from the fridge, needed some caffeine didn't have time to wait for coffee. I shut the door and got in my car. A 68 Mustang, not the best looking one in Phoenix but probably the fastest. I pulled out of River Street onto Central Avenue. River Street is in South Phoenix, its where I've lived most of my adult life.

My Dad bought it for my Mother on their 2nd. Anniversary, where they lived almost all their married life. They both been dead a few years now but in no way could I ever sell it. It was home.

Now about my name. Its Thomas Thomas, My Mother promised her father she would name me after him, his name was Thomas. How was she to know she would fall in love with a cop named Gene Thomas. She kept her promise so that's how I got the name, Thomas Thomas. It doesn't bother me, I don't know why it does others but it seems too.

I went north on Central to Jefferson took a left on 15th Ave to Monroe, three blocks away. There were several squad cars there along with Arkies old beat up pickup truck. I saw Lt. Van Buren before I got out of the car. He was chewing out Arkie about something, probably why I wasn't there yet. I got out and walked over to them. He looked at me with discuss in his eyes and voice, "so the two Thomas finally decided to show up, late night?"

I shrugged my shoulders. He grabbed my arm, well lets go see this one. The house was 1502 W. Monroe right on the corner. It had two downstairs bedrooms, and a third one on the second story. The owner Charles Ivan had made the top one into a small apt. The victim was in the first bedroom on the right as we entered. She like the other two was naked. Her pubic hair had been cut into a heart. Be cause of the pubic design the media had started calling him the "Valentine Killer" I didn't like that much. Give a killer a name makes him more famous.

There was no sign of rape. She had this look of expected sex right down to the time the killer had stuck an ice pick straight into her ear, right into her brain. And there was the note in her hand. It read "Today is the tomorrow you worried about yesterday." Three murders, three different notes. Was he just fucking with us or trying to show us up or trying to show how smart he was.

She died instantly. Several other cops were doing the fingerprint hair sample bit but I knew it was for nothing. This guy never left anything behind. The victims name was Faye Garcia, her roommate found her when she came home from work at Fry's a local grocer chain. They both were students at Phoenix College, a community college straight up 15TH Ave to Thomas about 3 miles away. I actually went there for about 15 minutes one time before Viet Nam came along. The roommate Reba Tubbs was in no condition to talk to us then. In fact I was worried she might freak out.

I told Van Buren we were going to the shop and would wait for him there. He didn't like it but gave his ok. We started to the shop,

Arkie following me in his truck. He pulled in and parked then got in the Mustang. We went for breakfast at Denny,s on 7th.Ave and Grand . We both order Grand Slams, with extra coffee.

As we ate he asked, "Ok you were with Bonnie last night, how was it?" My answer was, " I know Jerry was lost after Nina died, after all they were married 12years but him hooking up with Bonnie that I don,t understand." shit she's screwed half the cops in Phoenix and most of the ones in Tempe and Mesa. How was it, good.

We sat there eating and drinking till my phone went off. It was Van Buren, where in hell are you two? I'm getting gas for my car, cant follow leads down on an empty tank. He slammed the phone down, probably saw my car at Dennys as he went to the shop.

The police station is on Washington and 2nd Ave. right downtown. The detective squad is on the third floor. Below us is the small claims and juvenile courts. Above us the jail. There has been talk of moving it for years however there never seems enough money in the budget for it to happen.

The chief is Ryan Reynolds, red headed weighing about 280 all muscle and as nice or as nasty a person as you ever want to meet. He use to be a professional wrestler called "WILD RED REYNOLDS" a real bad guy. Don't ever tell him professional wrestling is fake, if you want to live.

I'm about 6 ft weigh 190 have sandy. grey hair and blue eyes. I'm an only child. My Dad use to say no matter how hard we tried we just couldn't make you a brother or sister.

Arkie is 5ft 9 or so weights 210 with almost no hair and a nice beer gut. He use to use the comb over style but got so much kidding about it just cut it all off. But don't kid yourself he gets more than his share of the ladies. Hes been married a few times with a few kids running around. They all love him and if hes late with the child support noone notices.

Me I tried marriage once. I think it lasted 2 months of which I was in Nam. I haven't tried it since. But to be honest it wasn't really her fault. We just didn't know each other. I was home on leave and horny she was looking for a meal ticket. I don't blame her for the divorce just wish she had waited till I got home, but that's all water under the bridge as they say.

The chief calls us in his office and said, "close the door." when he said that we knew someone was in for an ass chewing. He started with Lt. Van Buren, the got to us. It went on for 15 minutes, then he turned nice. Now the Mayor is coming at 3PM. For briefing and a short press conference. Make sure you all look presentable.

You, "he pointed at me" go get a haircut and shave, put on a suit. Look like you're a detective on my squad, I started to protest, but Chief its over 100 outside. You won't be outside plus you want to look good for your girlfriend the mayor don't you?

The mayor is Crystal Read. We both went to South Mountain Hi, graduated same class. I was the school jock, she was the school nerd. You know skinny, big glasses, no boobs, always carried a load of books and dressed like it was always winter with sweaters and such. But as they say boy has she changed. She now dresses very smart in fact to me it seems sexy, wears light blue contacts now and her figure would make a priest give up his vowel of chastity. And not to forget that little Cindy Crawford mole on her lip.

After high school she went to a university back east, worked for a big law firm and won some very big cases. When we had a federal case again us in Phoenix, she volunteered her services. She won the case saving Phoenix several million dollars. I went off to Viet Nam did my bit, came back to Phoenix and followed my Dad in being a cop. She decided to stay, run for mayor won with 91% votes. Running for her secong term now. Yes its true I like her a lot and she gives me those little winks once in a while but she's the mayor I'm just a cop. I can't see this going anywhere, plus I don't like the gossip going around about us.

He looked at Arkie and Van Buren you both could use a shave and a clean shirt and wear ties. That's it now get the hell out of my office. We left. Arkie said ,"we going to lunch first?" Then he added you got to buy, I'm hungry and broke and I'm late with my child support again. We went to "Petes Fish and Chips" on 27th Ave and Van Buren. I don't know how long Petes has been around but we use to go there after the Friday night football games. Same menu, same old building same everything but the price, its raised since but so has everything else. You order and pay at one window, pick up your order at the next one and set on picnic tables. No air conditioner, no fans and its usually busy. Pete figures its not broke don't fix it. I guess.

I dropped Arkie back off at the shop and went to the barber. I've used the same barber for years, A Mexican lady on 15th. Ave and Indian School Road. She don't speak a lot of English and my Spanish is sparse but she does it just like I like it without all that talk. Her name I think is Cora or Collettee something like that. She calls me Mr. Tomas. She has a lot children, usually one or more of them are there. They all speak excellent English. Her eldest daughter, Marie was there. She gave me a manicure. That took some time, I need to do that more often. Shit why not after all Crystal will be there.

I picked up my suit and some dress shirts at the cleaners. Took a long shower, used probably a little bit too much aftershave, got dressed. I looked in the mirror, not too bad. Not really GQ but Ok. I stuck an extra tie in my pocket for Arkie, I knew he wouldn't have one. Then I went to the shop. When I walked in, everyone gave me the wolf call. Detective Marilyn Marvin grabbed my butt. She's our only female dectective, really just one of the guys. We call her MM.

I went to my desk, pulled out what we know about the case, not much. I shuffled the papers hoping something would come to me, it didn't. Those notes bothered me. The first one said," Today is the first day of the rest of your life." The second was S.W.A.K. sealed with a kiss. Now this one "Today is the tomorrow you worried about yesterday' What in hell do they all mean?

It got quiet in the squad room. That usually meant someone important was there. She was behind me before I could turn around. I could smell her perfume "White Shoulders" I think it is. She put her hands over my eyes, guess who. I said, "cant be Arkie you don't smell like Coors." it's a little joke we play. She came in front of my desk then. I got to admit it. She almost takes my breath away every time I see her, but I tried to play it cool. I got up from my desk. Good afternoon your honor, nice to see you. I put out my hand to shake. She took it but just held it. She smiled, "my heart skipped a beat" come on Thomas you know me well enough to call me by name, don't you? I guess I blushed, I do that sometimes when shes around. Everyone laughed.

The Captain opened the door to his office, "what's all the racket about out here?" He walked over to Crystal and gave her a hug. She hugged back, its was like that with them. She said," I was just getting ready to tell Thomas how good he looks. Chief chuckled, yeah cleans up nice don't he?

Arkie and Van Buren came over. We went over what we were going to say in the press conference. Nothing really. Chief said," Ok lets do it." Crystal took my arm the others including the chief followed. Now our media room isn't much. About the size of a bedroom, with 12 chairs for the press, 4 or 5 chairs for us and a small podium. There was a smattering of applause as we entered. The chief went right to the mike. You all know the rules here, after we tell you all we know. You raise your hand and we answer your questions, if anyone shout out, its over OK? Heres what we know so far. He rambled on for a while not really saying anything.

Then he introduced the mayor. She gave a brief statement then introduced Lt. Van Buren as chief investigator and Arkie and me as the detectives on the case. Then she said, " any questions?" Patty McMahon Channel 5 said," I noticed as you entered you were holding Detective Thomas,s arm any truth to the rumor you two are romantically involved?" Crystal laughed, "we are here on a murder case and you ask that question?" As many of you know

Detective Thomas and I went to high school together and we are good friends. However if anything should happen you will be the first to know. Now anything else. A couple more people ask things we weren,t going to answer anyway. Then the chief said, " I know you all have deadlines for the 6 O Clock news so that's it for now, however if anything should happen, you will all know. Thank you for coming. They left and so did we.

Crystal took my hand on the way out, like we were holding hands or something. The chief, Van Buren and Arkie noticed. At my desk I said, "well your honor its been nice seeing you but I've got work to do." she winked OK Thomas be that way sometime it will happen bet on it. She turned and walked away. Everyones eyes followed her. Chief said, "get your asses busy, so they did."

Van Buren, Arkie and I went over the facts as we knew them. Three murders, all the ladies were nude, no sexual penetration, and all killed with ice picks something you could buy anywhere. In other words we had nothing. It was getting on 6 then, time to go home.

Arkie talked me into buying him dinner at Bill Johnsons Big Apple. it's a cowboy type of restaurant on East Van Buren St. Now East Van Buren is what we use to call "Hooker Heaven" but we have cleaned it up a lot. In fact a few of those ladies has given us some great leads on other more dangerous crimes so usually I just let them go unless some tourist turns in an official complaint.

Bill use to be a country DJ and did his show from the restaurant. Hes been dead a few years now and his son Bobby runs it now. The waitresses all dress western in jeans, cowboy shirts and wear six guns. The Bar B Que sandwiches are classics. Yes I buy his meals a lot. He was telling me on the way about a new girl working there he was trying to nail. I halfway listened.

As we pulled into the parking lot I noticed the mayors official car. I tried to chicken out but he said," surely your not going to let her make you miss dinner are you, what a pussy." I shook my head no, although to tell you the truth I wanted to see her then again. Arkie spotted his quest as we entered. He ask the hostess to seat us in her area. She said, "you mean Rose?" Yeah Rose, then to me I forgot her name. She sort of strutted over. Maybe 40 or so, big boobs and hips and jeans like second skin. A little too much makeup for me but she was exactaly Arkies type. She said, "well look at you, all dressed up with a tie and everything whats the occasion?" Arkie smiled just coming to see you Babe. He introduced me. She said, "your cute too, got a girlfriend?" Before I could answer she added, "your both so lucky the mayor is setting in the next booth." I looked, she wasn't there. Rose said," oh she not here now went to the little girls room." I started to get up. I was going to leave. She returned about then. Why Detectives Thomas and Arkie please join me. Arkie said, "Thomas saw your car in the parking lot and hoped we would see you here." she said," now Arkie you know better than to bullshit a bull shitter." They both laughed.

She scooted over and patted the seat beside her, I sat. We ordered and the talking started. I was surprised to know how much she remember from school, hell it was years ago. She remember my first car a 39 Lincoln Coupe. I bought it for $60. and painted it bright yellow. It did stand out. She even told about her and some other girls watching us take showers after a ball game. First time I never saw a naked man. Arkie said, "was it a BIG surprise Your Honor?" I thought so at the time but probably average. They laughed again, I think I blushed.

Thinking of that car brought back a lot of memories. After dinner I walked her out to her car. She kissed me lightly on the cheek. Thomas I don't know whats holding you back. You know I've always liked you from high school. You don't seem to really care about anyone special. Yes I hear all about the police groupies. I'm not going to sleep with someone I'm not going to marry but if you would like to go see the Suns or something sometime call me.

She said, "you know Thomas I hardly knew my father. He left me and Mom right after I was born. I only remember seeing him once. I was about 3, he had another little girl with him. Said it was my sister, called her Jade. Funny how I remember her name after seeing her only once all those years ago. We were told he went to Mexico and married a Mexican, had some kids with her. When I started to make a name for myself I wanted to look him up, but my mother said not too.

After she died I was really alone but I knew sometimes I would come home. She noticed my car. When are you going to wash that thing, I hope you keep your house better. She got in her car and left. I stood there a minute or two thinking. My car did look like shit and so did the house. I fished through my wallet for a card Marie Sanchez had given me. Shes a Mexican lady lives close to me that does house work, laundry etc. It read, "you make it dirty. I make it clean nothing in between." Phone 602-555-1934. I called her. I got her voice mail and left a message for her to come see me tonight if possible. It was just going on 9.

I took Arkie back to get his truck then started home. Thought better of it. Went to the Blakely station on Grand Ave. to get a car wash. The attention said," its pretty dirty man. " I'm not sure one wash will get it clean. So I said wash it again. Steam clean the engine too. He ask, " how about the junk in the car, old coffee cups, Mc Donald bags. Throw everything away. I want it showroom new. He smiled, shrugged his shoulders, spoke to the others working there.

I drank a coke and waited. It took the good part of an hour. When they were finished I hardly recognized it. I gave each one of them a generous tip. Ok now the house. Marie was setting on my front porch drinking a beer. I took her in the house, showed her around. I told her I want the place spotless like when my Mother was alive. I also said I wanted it done every week. Then I ask about a gardaner. Yes she knew someone could do it. I didn't ask what it would cost, I just said do it. As she was leaving she said, "Tomas" all the Mexicans call me that you getting married again or what?" I smiled and shook my head. Then in my mind I thought why not.

I slept like a baby that night, no wild dream or call outs from the squad, just those saying kept running through my mind. Now it we can just catch that bastard things would be good. I even though about calling Crystal to ask her for dinner but thought better of it-- easy boy. Just as I was leaving the house Marie pulled up in her car a pickup truck followed her. She introduced me to Jose, the gardner. I explained what I wanted him to do, especially about my Mothers roses. He smiled, no problem Senor Tomas. I make it beautiful. Again I didn't ask about the price. I got to start doing that.

I got to the shop and went straight to my desk. I didn't even get coffee. Arkie stumbled in a few minutes later. He grabbed two coffees and came over. Whats up? I said, " I might have an idea." I told him, " listen you have a calender here even on my desk, there are daily saying on them. Like Today is the first day of your life, and now Today is the tomorrow you worried about yesterday. Look at you name card, It says to serve and protect. And here I got this one last night, You made it dirty, I made it clean nothing in between. Maybe just maybe he works for the company who prints these things. Hell maybe hes the one who thinks them up.

We both got excited then. The chief saw something was going on and came out. I went over it all again to him. He listened, seems slim but hell we got nothing else whats the next move? I said," we need to get as many of the different sources of these things , shops that handle these things, stores that give calendars away with saying then see of any of the saying match up with the murder days. I looked at the chief, we need help on this. He called Shaw and Mayo over, explained what I needed. Said to me you got these guys for two days, and Thomas I dont want the Mayor to hear about this, got it. If it doesn't pan out I don't want to look the fool, understand. We all nodded.

We divided the valley into fourth , Shaw took the far east, Mesa, Apache Junction as far as Florence. Mayo the far West, out passed Maryville and even to Sun City. I had Arkie to take the east up to Tempe. I took the rest. I told them you heard the chief, we only got two days. So move as fast as you can, if there are duplicates take them better safe than sorry. Shaw and Mayo went out. Arkie hung back a little. I said, "Ok with up?" well last night after you left Rose picked me up and we went back to her place. We were looking at the calendar about setting up another date. Shes got one of those calendars with saying on them. I noticed the saying, "today is the first day of your life" on it. I thought it odd at the time but then forgot it.

Lets go over to Roses and get it, might help cant hurt. I motioned to Van Buren we were going out, after all he is the lead investigator. He nodded. As we got to the car Arkie said," was there a big storm last night I dont know about." why? Well your car is very clean. It wasn't when you left me. I explained about getting it washed and the house cleaned. Then he said, "and why the tie?" I had put one on that morning why I dont know. I said, " for my true love, any more questions?" He shook his head, just don't give the chief the idea we all need to start wearing them. I pulled it off and hung it from the rearview mirror.

Rose lived in a small trailer park on east McDowell close to the Motorola plant. We parked out front. Arkie gave that little knock. You know 3 short knocks then two more. She answered the door right away. She pulled the worn pink robe tightly around herself when she saw me. Arkie you should have called and told me you were bringing guest. He aint a guest its Detective Thomas you met last night. She ushered us inside. It was small but clean, there were several pictures of her on the walls and a plastic statue of Jesus in one corner. Probably a fallen Catholic was my guess.

Arkie explained why we were there. She said, "Oh I put it away after you left." Its on the top shelf in the kitchen. Here I'll help you get it. She pulled out a stepstool and climbed up. She smiled back at him. Better hold the stool it's a little rocky. Where he was standing he was looking straight up between her legs. She took her time finding it. I looked at the pictures and out the window. She handed the calendar to me. Here anything to help our men in blue. I thanked her and started to leave.

Arkie said, " can you give me a minute Thomas?' I nodded and left. I was in the car exactally ten minutes before he came bursting out the door. He was sweating and smiling. As we pulled onto Mc Dowell he said, " you know its funny, last night it was a small jungle there today smooth as a baby Why? I said, " your asking me about women, you got to be kidding. He messed with the radio till he found KOY they were playing "Why Do Fool Fall In Love."

We checked the date of the calendar with the first murder. The first saying was on the date of the first murder the others werent.I told the chief, well it's a start. Lets run with it he gave his ok.

We went to the Chili Bowl for lunch that day. it's a little joint about a block from the shop. Chili is all they serve with oyster crackers along with drinks. The chili is rated Nino, children "not very hot" Mamas "a little hotter and Big Daddy " hot as hell" just touching it to your lips and your eyes and nose starts to water. We both got Nino with milk to drink. Drinking milk is smart with chili, it soothes it somehow. I tried Big Daddy once and shit fire for three days, never again. My phone rang, it was Crystals secretary Janice wanting to know if I was available to see her honor later that day. The mayor has something she would like to discuss with you about the case. I told her the chief would have to approve any thing about the case or any meeting. She said he already had. The mayor will expect you about 8, and Thomas she said, "have a good time" then hung up before I had time to say anything.

Hell is everyone trying to fix me up with the mayor. I told Arkie about the call. He smiled. I knew about that already. Man sometimes you are slow. We went back to the shop, I went in to see the chief. What in the hell is this all about. He got up from his desk came around and hugged my shoulder. Thomas the mayor got a strange message on her phone last night. I want you to go there and see what going on, see if she is in danger or not. As you know she got a lot of strange messages, threats even when she put Alex Zapata away for murder.

Maybe its nothing. I think its nothing or I would have called you earlier, but just to be sure go check it out. And I'm sure you could sure a nice dinner with her alone. He raised his hands in protest no I'm not trying to fix you up just take it as it is OK? After all she is the mayor and we took an oath to serve and protect. Plus I like that gal a lot. Shes got more balls that half of the street cop in Phoenix.

I left the shop early and went home. Jose was working his ass off, and the yard was looking good especially Moms roses. When I entered the house all I could smell was Pine Sol. I finally found Marie bent over the bathtub. She was entirely wet and the shorts and tee shirt she was wearing were almost see thru. I coughed as I entered. She didn't both to cover up. Tomas this place is really dirty but when I finish you can bring your girlfriend home, that's what you wanted aint it?

But you are home now, so I stop and come back tomorrow OK? I nodded. She gathered up her cleaning stuff and left. She took the gardner with her. I drank a beer, cooled off then showered and dressed to go see Crystal. It was way too early so went to Christown to the movies. That should kill a couple of hours. As I was waiting to get my popcorn a girl approached me. You Detective Thomas? I said I was. I saw you on TV with the mayor, she your girlfriend? I said just an old friend. She called a boy over. This is Ricky Adams, my boyfriend. We got a bet your sleeping with her, who wins. I said No one. That's personal. The boy laughed. It was a high girly giggle really. Them I looked at him. He was about 5ft. 10 with the smoothest complexion I had ever seen, his eyes were a funny almost golden color "contacts I thought" he had small effeminate hands with long nails, and short curly hair. In fact he was a lot prettier than the girl he was with. He said to the girl who he called Shirley, in that effeminate voice. I don't think the policeman likes us very much. Not as much as we like him anyway. Then he grabbed her hand and they went inside. At the door he turned and I swear to God he winked at me.

I wasn't interested in the movie by then so went across the street and played pool for a couple of hours. I left just as the movie was letting out. At the red light on 19th. Ave they were beside me, She was driving. She honked the horn and waved like we were old friends. He winked again. The light changed, I turned left they went straight ahead thank God. But his face remained in my mind. Strange looking guy all right. I got to Crystals a few minutes early.

She met me at the door wearing a pale pink out fit that showed off her curves nicely. She handed me a glass of fresh lemonade. My housekeeper made it especially for you tonight. She led me out on the screened in porch with the bar b que built in at the end. There were steaks and a nice salad setting on the table with chips and salsa. She said, " I don't use it much but when visitors come from back east they expect bar b que steaks, you know cowboy style."

I lit the grill, it was gas with mesquite logs, really western you know. I ask how she liked her steak. A little pink inside, my taste too. I said ," before we get eating I want to hear that tape." she brought out the machine to the porch. She said," maybe its nothing, you know I'm running for reelection." Maybe just someone whos not going to vote for me. The tape started and then in that voice I recognized right away. He said," giggling," Politicians are like diapers they need to be changed sometimes." I played it again. Yes it was the strange boys voice from the movies, Ricky Adams.

She was hugging me from behind. Well what do you think? I said, "probably nothing he was giggling when he said it but I,ll look around." She said,"the steaks are ready, lets eat." As we were eating I drank a couple more glasses of lemonade, Crystal drank water. She went into get dessert. When she returned I was almost asleep. I told her I didn't feel good and was going home. She insisted I laid down on the couch for a while first. I just kicked off my boots and laid down on the porch swing. She got a pillow, put it on her lap and rested my head on it. It would have been sexy if I wasn't feeling so bad.

I drifted off then woke with a start. Crystal wasn't there and I heard a noise out by my car. I pulled my gun, "of course I had it with me" and rushed out toward the car. I heard two loud pops, felt a burning in my stomache. I knew I had been shot, Id felt that pain before in Nam. One had just grazed me but the other one got me pretty good. Crystal rushed out screaming. I said call 911. I already have, their on the way. I thought shit I,ve got blood all over her nice outfit. I blanked out.

When I came to, Arkie and the chief were there. The medics was putting me in the bus. They all climbed in with me. The next thing I remember is being in a bed covered with grey blankets. There were wires and tubes running from various parts of my body. I could hear the moniter ticking away. A white ghost seemed to float above and around me.

I Blacked Out.

I woke screaming in pain, the ghost and someone else came injected a blue fluid in my arm.

I Blacked Out Again.

It went on like that for a while. I don't know how long I was there just hanging on. As you may know a stomache shot is one of the worse you can get. Just too many organs. The pain would come and then nurse and the white ghost would appear and inject me with the blue liquid and I would.

Black Out Again.

I woke one morning and the moniter was off, the tubes and wires were out of my body. Crystal was setting there in a chair. Arkie and the chief was standing by the door. Arkie spoke first, " Ok man you had enough vacation, we got work to do so get your ass out of bed." The chief come over and just squeezed my shoulder with that ham of a hand of his. Crystal was crying all over the place.

Arkie said, "why in hell were you taking zxyan?" You system was full of it. Zxyan I never heard of the stuff, you know I never even take aspirin. You had enough in you to make you sleep for a day or two, maybe forever. The light bulb above my head snapped on. It had to be in the lemonade. I drank three glasses, Crystal drank water that must be it. She said the housekeeper had made it specially for me before she went home.

I took Crystals hand, what do you know about her? She came with the house. I needed a housekeeper, she had worked for the previous mayor before, so I just had her stay on. I started to get out of bed. The chief said, "wait a minute hoss, you are to stay in bed for at least two more weeks." As you may remember you just got shot twice. Your not healed up enough to go back to work.

The mayor has arranged for you to a have nurses around the clock. You can go home but only on those provisions. I laid back down. Crystal spoke," you can stay at my place if you want to I have plenty of room and my phone system is directly hooked to the police station. How about the housekeeper? She ask for two weeks off yesterday, something about a family emergency in Texas. I hesitated. She said," I wont take no for an answer, now I'm going to leave so you can get dressed." I'll wait for you in the lobby.

I told the chief and Arkie about the strange boy from the movies. I was sure his voice was the one I heard on the tape. I gave them his name and description and ask them not to let anyone by that I meant Crystal know what was going on. Arkie said, "Im going to get that motherfucker and the housekeeper too." Hell who would buy my lunch for me if they got you? He was sort of snuffling around. I kicked him and the chief out and got dressed.

A pretty Mexican nurse helped me. She said, "Senor Tomas my auntie is Marie Sanchez she said to tell you the house is OK she will take care of it while you are gone, no money. Jose has your

Mothers roses looking great maybe she will bring you some. I just nodded, these are good people. They put me in a wheelchair and took me to where Crystal and the media were waiting. I didn't know they would be there. They took a thousand pictures and ask a thousand questions. Crystal said, "when Detective Thomas is well enough he will talk to you but right now its rest. And before you ask and the gossip starts he will be staying with me. Now that that's settled please let us by. Janice , Crystals secretary was waiting in the car.

They got me to her home and put me in the den on the ground floor. The bedrooms were on the second floor, but they had changed the den and make it into a bedroom for me. It was a lot nicer than my place but it didn't feel like home. One of the nurses was waiting. Her name was Stella, she was also one of auntie Marie nieces. I don't know how many nieces there are but all my nurses were Maries relatives.

Crystal hung around for a while but finally she said," sorry Thomas but I've got to go." There is a rally tonight at Encanto Park for me and James Nelson, you knew he was running against me didn't you. Anyway I've got to be there. The nurse will cook you something when you get hungry and be sure you take your medicine. She kissed me on the cheek, the nurse was watching. After Crystal left the nurse said, "Ok Tomas what do you want to eat?" I said a big cheeseburger, no onion and a beer. She frowned. No beer doctors orders. No beer? Ok just one but you not say anything OK. I promised I wouldn't. She went in the kitchen to cook.

I pulled the phone over to my bed and called Arkie. He had a message from some guy in New York who wanted me to call him. He would only speak to me. There is three hours difference in New York and Arizona, I thought he might be in so I called. The operator answered, New York Attorney General Office, how may I direct your call. I gave her the extension number. The voice that answered was very mascline, very rich type. This is Jonathon

Rogers how may I help you. I told him who I was. Them he become very buddy buddy. Thomas good to hear from you. Heard you had a close call.. You OK now? You know I went to law school with your mayor, she spoke of you often. Then he got right to it. I've been following your case very closely, I think I might be able to help you. We had a case just two nights ago in the Village, the M/O same as yours. College girl, stripped nude, close to having sex, ice pick in the ear and her pubic hair cut into a heart. There was also a note in her hand it read, " Happy days are here again." Maybe your killer has traveled east, from your district to mine. Is it possible for you and your partner to come here so we can work on it together. Of course our office will bear all the expenses. I said I'd get back to him and hung up.

The phone rang then, it was Arkie. Theres been another one. Happened maybe three or four days ago. The roommate came home and found the body. Just like the others the message this time said, "Wake up and smell the roses." She had been to Prescott for the weekend with friends. And her other roommate was gone left a message she was traveling with her boyfriend. Was going back east to see her parents and Ricky needed some time just to get away. Guess who the boyfriend is, Ricky Adams.

I told him about the New York call. He said, " so whats next?" I said were going, don't give me any shit about two weeks more rest. Lets go get this son of a bitch. Then I called the chief and told him the same thing. He just grunted, I knew we couldn't keep you in bed for two weeks. I'll have your travel arrangements made, so you can leave tomorrow. Your at least get one night rest. Have you told Crystal yet? No. Better do it easy boy shes about ready to break. I said I would and hung up. I dozed off.

The next thing I knew Crystal was setting beside my bed holding my hand. A very cold cheeseburger sat on the night stand. I told her about the call from New York and Jonathon Rogers. Her face got a cold look then, yes he wanted to be my beau that's all nothing happened. When was the last time you heard anyone called a beau? She gave me my pills then pulled the chair over as close to my bed as she could get. I'm sleeping here in case you need anything in the night. I said but you have a nurse here. I let her go home. I want to take care of you. Now go to sleep. I was almost out when she climbed upon the bed and pulled me close to her. In a whisper she said," Thomas I love you."

I woke to the smell of bacon cooking. I had slept the night through and needed to go to the bathroom very badly. I dropped my legs over the side of the bed and holding on to other furniture. I made it to the john. I noticed blood was oozing from under one of my bandages. And I hurt like hell. I wondered if I really could make the trip to New York today. I got back into bed just as she entered with my breakfast, toast with orange marmalade, bacon 2 strips, sausage 2 links, 2 eggs over easy, a large oj and a glass of milk. I said, "what no coffee?" The doctor said no caffee for a while, not when your on the pain medication. I ask, "where yours?" I already had my breakfast. I,ve got to go to the office. The nurse will help you with anything you need.

She kissed me, a little longer this time and not on the cheek. She told the nurse, make him stay in bed and rest. She answered with a smile. "Yes mam." As soon as Crystal left I called Arkie. Our tickets ready. We leave at 6PM, you need to call the New York guy to pick us up. Any news on Ricky and his traveling companion. No, but listen to this the mayors housekeeper use to be Eve Zapata, Alex Zapata ex-wife. His ex-wife I said. Wait, wait it gets better some say she was really his sister not his wife. Nice family huh. She married the Adams guy and changed her name two months after Alex went to prison. And another thing Mr. Adams died suddenly 3 weeks after the wedding. Maybe were looking at a Black Widow here. I said, " pick me up at 5 and you better pack a very light bag we might be there a day or two. He started to hang up. Listen Arkie, I'm bleeding a little. I'm going to have the nurse repack the wound. I might need to lean on you a little. He said, "shit I been leaning on you for years no problem.

And Arkie, "Don't tell anyone else about this Ok. You think I'm a fuckin snitch? See you at 5. Oh the hell with it I'm coming over now. I called the nurse in. I need some clothes, maybe you can call Marie to bring me some. She smiled but Tomas there is a lot of mens clothes in the second bedroom. They all look new maybe some of them will fit you? I wonder why she would have mens clothes, left over by an ex lover I hoped not.

Arkie came bursting in. I told the chief I was coming to see you. He just saluted so I left. I told him the nurse was looking for something for me to wear, go help her. They were both gone about 10 minutes but returned carrying a bunch of new clothes. Arkie said, " Thomas the second bedroom is full of clothes, all your size whats going on? Even new boots and shit from Goldwaters, I know you cant afford them. I shrugged my shoulders. The nurse said, " you are bleeding too much, I cant stop it better go to the hospital." I shook my head. We ve got to go to New York today. She said, " you are crazy, no way can you travel." I got up from the bed and started to get dressed. I felt faint, I realized my cape and the big S on my chest were disappearing. I'm not Superman after all.   I passed out.

I woke up in Doctors Hospital on Camelback Rd. Crystal, Arkie and the chief were all there. They all gave me hell along with my doctor. I said, "but I've got to go to New York today. Our killer is there and I've got a line on him. It took a while but they talked me into staying in bed. I don't think I could have gotten out anyway but damn it sometimes I'm really stubborn. Right then I wanted nothing more than to get that S.O.B. Arkie called Jonathon Rogers in New York and explained the situation. He understood and said when I'm able to travel he was ready to help. In the meantime he would keep me advised of any new developments. He ask about Crystal. Arkie said she was Ok then hung up. S.O.B. don't need to know about your true love man.

I obeyed the doctors and everyone else for two days, I was hurting but I was going crazy just laying there. The chief allowed

Arkie, Shaw, Mayo and Van Buren to bring me some files and keep me advised on the case, but he said," you get out of that bed I personally will kick your ass." He didn't smile when he said it.

As Shaw and Mayo were looking for the calendars they also picked up the year books from the schools. I ask for them first. I wanted to see if Ricky Adams was going to school with any of the victims. I found Richard Adams going to bible college. The Unified Theoligy Academy of Arizona on west Bethany Home Road, close to where I saw them at the movies. But then I found Ricky Adams going to Phoenix Community College on 15th Ave and Thomas close to where we found the third body. He was studying Drama under John Paul.

Twins, we were dealing with twins. Were they both killers? I called the chief, said I need to talk to him in person, yes I was still in bed. But secretly one of the nurses another of Maries nieces had been getting me up walking the corridors at night. I felt pretty good. Not good enough to wrestle an alligator yet but better. The chief come blustering in, he doesn't go anywhere quietly. From his inside pocket he handed me a Coors. One beer aint going to kill you just drink it before the doc comes in. I did, I think two big gulps was all it took.

Then I told him about the twins or what I thought might be the twins. Hell it might be the same guy using two different names. He called Shaw and Mayo to go check them out. He said," now you been here almost a week now, when you getting out?" I started to tell him right now. Hes phone rang. What! Keep her there I'm coming. He said," can you believe it that bitch the house keeper Mrs. Adams just showed up at the mayors place. Acted like nothing had happened. I dropped my legs over the bed. I said," wait for me I'm coming too." He shook his head. Stay here I'll come right back and tell you all that's going on. I ask," what about Crystal?' She wasn't home, don't worry. She,s safe. She is out running for office. Don't worry Thomas I sent MM with her. From now on till the election MM will be with her any time shes in public. I though she better be, but you know I still wondered about all those mens clothes at her place. Good thing I'm not the jealous type or am I?

Lt. Van Buren came in then he said, " Arkie and the chief just arrested Mrs. Adams. They are booking her in. They will be here soon. You know Thomas I was really pissed at you for sleeping with Bonnie. Then I found out she was sleeping with any one who had a dick, please except my apoligies. He stuck out his hand, I took it. We shook. I said, " sorry anyway Jerry I shouldn't have done it." No problem. The chief and Arkie came in laughing like hell. Whats the matter I ask? You wont believe this. She starting talking about her boys on the way to the station. Of course Arkie had to ask her about the pubic hair designs. She flipped up her dress. There under a flab of fat hanging almost to her knees she showed it off. Her pubic hair was cut into a heart shape. And the smell. I've smelt skunks that smelled better. It almost gagged me. I ask her why. She said, "well a boys got to have a hobby don't he," I let him practice on me.

I said, "someone call Jerry Springer we got a show for him." She might be the sister of Alex Zapata, had two sons by him. One is studying to be a minister, the other to be an actor. They are probably killers and one is a pubic hair designer. Hell Jerry could make a week of shows from them.

Then the chief got serious. Ok Lt. Van Buren, what's your next move? Jerry shook his head like he didn't know. I said, "well get me out of here and let me and Arkie go to New York and run that down." We might turn up the killer or killers who knows? Two more days, you got to stay here at least two more days so the doc says. Then well see. But I think for now we get the worse picture of Mrs. Adams we can take, put it on the front page of the paper saying she has been arrested in connection with the Valentine killings. Maybe we will spook one of them into doing something stupid. I ask, "if Crystal knew about the arrest?" No, not yet but she will in a minute or two when you phone her. He handed me his phone. I called. She answered the phone crying. Thomas whats going wrong in my life. I tried to help the lady giving her a job and she tried to kill you. I told her to come see me, we would talk about it.

Shaw and Mayo came in the room was getting full. A doctor stuck his head in the door, no more visitors. The chief nodded. Shaw said, "man you wont believe this." When I went to the bible school they said a Richard Adams wasn't enrolled there. So I showed them the picture in the year book. The receptionist got very nervous ask me to wait and went into one of the offices. A little "Jimmy Swagger" came strutting out. He ask if I was there about the suicide. I said yes. He went on poor boy committed suicide by sticking an ice pick straight into his brain. He must have really been desperate. You know only the Lord knows when your time is up. Suicide is a terrible sin, he sort of bowed his head then. Right after he had changed his name too, seemed strange to me. However you boys in blue probable see things like this all the time. I ask him about the name change. Why he changed it to Richard Read, said the double R was good luck. So now hes got an ID saying his name was the same as the mayor, and he commits suicide like the girls were killed. This case is getting stranger and stranger all the time. I looked at the chief, so which one is really dead is it Richard or Ricky using the Read last name. Does the girl, Shirley Waters know who she really traveling with or is she dead somewhere nude with an ice pick in her brain. God its getting confusing. Crystal came in then with the doctor.

He shooded Shaw and Mayo out of the room. Told the others they had 5 more minutes that's all. The doc and Crystal went over in the corner for a confab. They keep looking at me. I though what in the hells going on, what do they have in their minds now. They came over to my bed. The doc picked up my chart from the end of the bed and looked it over closely. Crystal was holding my hand and softly talking to me. The doc said, " the mayor has convinced me to release Mr. Thomas in her custody. As long as he agrees to stay in bed for another 5 days at least. She also has nurses arranged for him around the clock and of course I will make house calls every other day. I though house calls, what doctor makes house calls in this day and age.

Being the mayor does have its privilages. I looked at Arkie, he shrugged his shoulders. I said, "Ok I'll agree to this if on the fifth day Arkie and I can go to New York and get this settled, providing there are no new murders. If there are I'm out of that bed and on the job, understand? Crystal said," of course darling, right Red. The chief looked like he wanted to kill someone, "maybe me" but he said yes. I wish she hadn't called me that in front of everyone. I said," I've got to go to my place and get some thing and I needed Arkie to help me. She said," of course." The chief said Ok.

They got a wheel chair and took me out to her waiting car. They bundled me in back with Crystal. Arkie and the driver were up front. There wasn't any conversation on the way home. As we pulled up in front of the house, Marie came running out. Jose had the roses looking great, my Mother would have approved. I introduced her honor. Marie said. " I've know Crystal a long time, same as you." Arkie helped me into the house. It was spotless. Crystal said," its just like I remember it. ' you remember it, when were you ever here. Don't you remember on your 16th birthday you invited the entire homeroom class. I was here then. I even went in your room. The walls were covered with sport stars and there was an old Playboy magazine under your bed. Arkie looked at me like whats going on. I shrugged, hell I didnt know. We got a few things but mostly I just wanted to go home for a few minutes and see what it looked like clean again. And I found out another thing about Crystal I didn't know. I was beginning to feel like she was stalking me, but why?

On the ways to Crystals place Arkie told me Jonathon from New York had called twice. Just to check on me and let us know there was nothing new on his end of the investigation. He keeps asking about Crystal too. She overheard this and got a grim look on her face. Something going on there I don't know about?Crystal and the nurse got me settled in my room "the den." I noticed a larger bed had been put in, I think it was a Queen size now. I said I need to talk to Arkie in private, Police business. I told him I was still worried about the clothes in the second bedroom. I needed him to take a second look and let me know whats going on. He nodded. Later when Her Honor goes to speak at a rally in Encanto Park.

He told Crystal he was going back to the shop, he would give her a ride back to her office where MM would pick her up for the rally. She said Ok. She gave the nurse some instruction especially about my medicine and absolutely NO beer. The nurse said, " of course not your honor She kissed me goodbye again. I'm beginning to like it more and more.." Arkie said, see you later hoss and they left. I turned on the TV to channel 5, Patty McMahon was telling about the arrest of Mrs. Adams, she knew just how to make it seem really bad. Showed the picture the chief had picked out several times. Then added Detective Thomas is now resting at the home of Her Honor Mayor Read. She added with a wink, I think there is more to this story. Patty Mc Mahon for channel 5 news now back to our regular programming. I turned it off and went to sleep.

Yes I'm feeling better but I get tired easily. When I woke Arkie was setting there drinking a beer. He handed it to me, I took a swig. He said, "hoss I already looked again upstairs. I found your old year book. She had the pages with your pictures on them covered so they wouldn't dry out. I don't know if she is obsessed with you or just plain nuts. I ask him if he still had the travel vouchers for New York? He said, "we,re going aint we?" I nodded, tomorrow night when Crystal has that debate with James Nelson on TV. It will run late she wont be home before midnight by that time we'll be on the plane. I said," you need to call Jonathon and give him our arrival time, and ask him to pick us up. Just take one change of clothes. Dress cowboy style after all that's what they will expect. After all we're the gunslingers from Arizona. Probably ask us about Tombstone and the fight at the OK Corral.

The nurse came in gave me my medicine, then handed me a bottle of mouthwash. I guess I looked funny. She said I can smell the beer.So I swished it away. I was asleep again when Crystal got home. I heard her talking to the nurse when told her to get some rest. She would set with me for a while. I sort of dozed off again. The next thing I felt was her slipping in bed with me. I could feel her bare skin rubbing against me. I started getting an erection. I wanted too but I couldn't . She said," that's Ok honey, I,ve waited to have sex a long time I can wait a little longer. No man has ever touched me there. I even had only women doctors so I would be a virgin when I come to you. Go to sleep now we both can wait till your better. I lay there a while her nude body against me, till I finally passed out. Man I must not feel good, a virgin laying against me and I go to sleep. I'm going to blame it on the medicine.

When I woke up later to go to the bathroom she was gone. She came in the morning about 6 bringing me medicine and some toast with a glass of OJ. She also brought me a small cup of decaf coffee. She winked now don't tell the doctor I gave you that, our little secret right. I nodded it wasn't really coffee but better than nothing. I needed to rest a lot today because tonight Id need all my strength to fly to the Big Apple. Crystal came back later carrying a dress bag. She said, "I wont be home at all till tonight so I'm taking a change of clothes with me. Now I want you to stay in bed and rest. I'll call you later. Watch me on TV tonight, please. I told her I wished her good luck although I knew she didn't need it. She said, " were getting closer, you and I right? I nodded. She give me the biggest kiss yet. Yes I like it.

Thirty minutes after she left Arkie got there. He handed me the travel vouchers. I said, " first class we're traveling first class." Does the chief know about this? He will soon as we get back, don't sweat it. After we solve this case and he retires who do you think the mayor will promote to be the new chief? You lover boy, who else? I ask if he had called Jonathon about our arrival time. Yeah I left a message with his secretary. Got a real sexy voice, have to see if the rest matches. He started up the stairs how John Wayne do you want to go? All the way I said. He came down carrying an arm load of clothes, pick out what you want, I did.I picked out a western style shirt with snap buttons. jeans, Tony Lama boots, and a silver belt buckle with a flag of Arizona on it. There were even socks and jockeys in my size.

Arkie handed me a new Stetson, I put it on a little too big. Arkie said, "ok that ones mine, I'll go get you another. I said, "how many are there?" A lot. He finally found one I liked that fit me. The phone rang. It was Crystal. Just wanted to say hello, and ask how you are feeling. I'm Ok just resting. I,ll let you go. Get plenty of rest. I love you. I hung up quickly before I had to say something I wasn't sure about.

Arkie said, "lets leave early just in case someone gets nosy." He told the nurse if her honor calls again just say he is sleeping and better you let him rest. She smiled, "Ok Senor Arkie I will tell lie for you. By the way Senor Arkie my auntie Marie said she think you very sexy. Arkie said, "I'll call her when we get back with the killer. She smiled again. He nudged me. I still got it hoss.

We got to the airport 4 hours too early but that's how Arkie wanted it. We went into the first class lounge and watched TV till it was boarding time. Arkie drank several beers, I just had one light Coors. On the plane he put away a few more. I was in a little pain so just popped the pills with water. I passed on the dinner although to tell you the truth I was hungry. I was just afraid something stupid would happen. The plane arrived at 12:45 AM New York time. A man in a very expensive suit was holding a card with our names on it. He introduced himself. It was Jonathon Rogers. He had on a $1000. suit, with a custom tailored shirt, gold cuff links, a gold Rolex and a diamond pinkie ring. We looked like the poor relatives beside him.

Arkie nudged me. This your brother from another mother? We did look a little a bit alike. Same size, same hair same weight, same old high school football jock walk. I've been kidded about it lots of times. But he was very nice, spoke about some other cases Arkie and I had worked on. His car of course was a BMW, make my Mustang looked again like the poor relative. He had put us up at the Sheridan, telling the manager who he knew by name to give us the VIP treatment. Telling him we were working on an important case together. We got settled in our rooms, telling us he would pick us up at 10AM if that was OK with us. He could only give us that day, he had to go to a conference in New Orleans. He would leave in the afternoon.

Our rooms were adjoining room. Arkie said, "shit this room is bigger than my house." I agreed. I said" well I hate to do this but I've got to call Crystal, I shouldn't have left without telling her." Arkie said I'm going to listen in on the extension. The nurse answered, boy you are in deep shit. Crystal got on the horn, "yes what do you have to say for yourself. Don't you know I worry about you. You are not well enough to go back to work. The only thing I could say was, "sorry." she said, : Ok its too late now, get back as soon as you can, then she added Arkie I know you are listening I blame you for all this." Your going to be walking a beat in South Phoenix if anything goes wrong got it? Then she said, "go to bed I love you." With out hesitation I said I love you too. She laughed about time you said it. We both hung up.

We got a beer from the mini bar and sat talking. I don't know what kind of beer it was but it surely wasn't Coors. I told him what Crystal had told me about being a virgin. He said, 'all that meat and no potatoes, man you don't know how lucky you are. You a got a girl crazy about you, maybe a little obsessive. Shes the mayor, got a few bucks, bought you all those clothes, can promote you to chief and is a virgin on top of all that, and your worried about it. Lord help me this boy is nuts.

We finally passed out for a few hours. I woke with Arkie singing in the shower. I tenderly got out of bed. I called down for breakfast for us both. He came out wearing a robe with the hotels name in it, saying I'm taking this home. No matter what they say. The breakfast came. Two eggs over easy, two pieces of toast, two small pieces of bacon and coffee $22.95 each. Shit in Phoenix I can eat breakfast for a week on that. I signed the bill. The boy stood there holding out his hand. I ask him wouldn't the breakfast be on our finale bill. Yes sir, everything but the tip. I ask him isn't it your job to bring the food to the room and didn't he get paid for doing it. Yes sir was his reply. Then what is the tip for? You only brought it up, you didn't cook anything did you. He hurried out the door muttering to himself something about those fucking cowboys. So much for New York hospitality.

We started to eat, shit the coffee was even cold. I told Arkie when we get to the office to act western. What's that? Never mind just be yourself. I took two "Atomic Bomb" pain pills before we left the room. Arkie said we better call the chief before we go see Jonathon. I agreed. The chief answered on the first ring. He wasn't happy. He said, " listen you yahoos, I got some funny maybe bad news. " We ran another check on Mrs. Adams she just wouldn't stop talking seems she was married before she got involved with Zapata. Her husband was Richard Read, the mayors father. I don't know what this means but I don't think its good. You guys get back here as soon as you can. He hung up without saying goodbye. Oh shit. We were waiting in the lobby when Jonathon pulled up in a cab. I ask about his car. Oh I only use it on weekends or late at night too much traffic in the daytime. I garage it close to the office. Costs me a fortune but you know that's New York. I think we both nodded at the same time. You can't even keep your car at your house. You got to pay for a place to park it does that seem right to you?

Any way when we got to the office it was if we were visiting royalty. He introduced us all around as the cowboy detectives from

Arizona. Here to help him on a case he as working in conjunction with the Phoenix Police Department. All the men were dressed in either dark blue or grey suits with striped or red ties. The women too worn dark skirts and white blouses but I think a few of them had forgotten their bra, I saw a lot of nipples straining to get free. We went into his private office. His secretary brought in coffee. Ask how we liked it. Arkie said just like we like our women straight and strong. She blushed.

After the coffee ordeal was over we finally got to business. He ask about my health. Said I was a little pale. To tell the truth I was in pain but said, "I'm Ok lets get this done." He showed us the pictures of the crime scene, yeah it looked like our right down the hair design and the note. He had told us before he had to leave that day so just left the evidence with us and went on about his business. I said to Arkie, "you ever leave the evidence with someone else." No fucking way. I'm not to happy being here are you? I shook my head no. We got copies of everything via his secretary who seems to me to be always around.

I said lets get out of here this has been a waste of time and money. His secretary came rushing in. You have a call from your chief in Phoenix, you can take it here. Just push number 9. Arkis pushed number 8 by mistake. I started to say something. He held up his hand for silence. His face got very red. Then he pushed number 9. The chief said, Thomas I got bad news as Crystal was doing campaigning in Chris Town, she had to pee. MM checked out the john just two girls doing their makeup. Crystal said, no problem. We waited a good ten minutes. MM went in one of the girls was dead and Crystal was gone. Shes been kidnapped. I said were on our way home. I told Arkie what the chief said. He exploded that Son Of A Bitch. When I pressed the wrong button Jonathon was on the line he was talking to Ricky Adam telling him they would met in New Orleans just as planned and too be sure and bring his sister Crystal with him.

I ask Jonathons secretary where he was. He left a few minutes ago. Took our private jet. I ask where he was staying in New Orleans? She sort of raised her eye brows. You know About his trip there ? Of course he just forgot to give us his hotel in case we need to talk to him again. She wrote the name on one of her cards and gave it to Arkie. In case your ever in New York again my private number is on the back, call me sometime.

We rushed out of office and grabbed a cab to the airport. Arkie said, "how about our clothes and shit." I said fuck it I'll buy you new stuff. We were lucky and got a flight out in an hour. I called the chief from the airport telling him what we now knew about Ricky, Jonathon, and Crystal being Ricky sister. I drank why too much on the plane. The pain pill and the booze didn't work well together. I felt like hell sick but not sick enough to puke.

I stated thinking, here was the girl I had thoughts of marrying, being the mother of my children and her brother is the killer of at least four ladies we knew about and he has some odd connection with Jonathon in New York and now she is kidnapped by him, or is she really? Does she know all about whats going on and how is she really connected to it all. Did she know her housekeeper was really her stepmother. And who shot me?

The housekeeper said it wasn't her or Ricky and she seemed like a woman who liked to boost. I was so glad when the plane finally landed at Sky Harbor. The chief and Van Buren were there to meet us. He wasn't too happy about my condition and I wasnt too happy he had let Crystal get kidnapped. We declared a closed war. As usual he blamed Arkie for not taking better care of me. I said, "listen you can fire me today but shut your fucking a hole unless you have some good news about your investigation on Crystal. " His not my baby sitter, I do what I want when I want. He looked at me like something he would wipe his ass on, I've seen that look before.

We went to the shop. I knew when this case was closed so was my time on the force. Probably made a big announcement on TV about how he was sorry to see me go but I had decided on early retire, he wished me well. I've also seen him do that before. When we entered the squad room MM come up to me crying. Sorry Thomas my fault. I said no its his fault hes the chief at least for now. The room got very quiet. I got to learn to keep my mouth shut sometimes. The telephone operator signaled I had a phone call. I answered in the usual way. Detective Thomas here how may I help you. It was Crystal. Thomas I'm sorry. The phone was taken from her. Thomas this is Ricky Adams remember me? We met at the movies remember. I said I did. Well my sister and I are going to New Orleans to meet my real first love, you know him Jonathon Rogers. I don't know why but he wants me to bring her too. Anyway I was to tell you if anyone tried to stop us in anyway I m going to kill her right then and there.

I ask why New Orleans? Well if you must know we are going to open a club there. A club, what kind of a club? You know for special people like us. I said you mean murders? Murders no silly, just special people. He even let me name it. Really whats it going to be called. Ricky House of Unusual Pleasure. What do you think. I said that's a great name all right. I was trying to keep him on the phone for a trace. His voice got very soft then. Do you really mean it. You know if we had met in different circumstances I bet be could have been friends. I said no doubt in my mind. Well he said I better go now it's a long drive and Jonathon don't want me to drive too fast and get pulled over for speeding. I said Ok but you promised I could talk to Crystal before you hang up. Did I well Ok but just for a minute. I said now remember Ricky you are not to hurt Crystal in any way Jonathon wants her in New Orleans.

He handed the phone to her She was still crying. I said, " snap out of it, I'm going to get you out of this somehow. Just be as calm as you can be. Now say Goodbye and say you will see me in New Orleans. She did. Ricky came back on the phone. Now remember Thomas no one is suppose to stop us on the way or you know what I'm suppose to do. I said before you go I need to know something.

Sure I feel like were friends now. Why the messages? He laughed a high cackle. That was just to confuse you, Jonathon had that idea. I said well it worked. I'm hanging up now. Wait one more minute what car are you driving. I need to know so I can tell the police not to bother you.

He hesitated, well Ok its, Shirley car she don't need it anymore I ask why. You know, don't you. He said this time I'm really hanging up. I said no problem, have a nice trip. We both hung up. I looked at the operator. He shook his head. No trace calling from a disposable cell phone.

We looked up Shirley Waters car, it was an old Honda, tan in color with Arizona license SWC 112 personal plate. Should be easy to spot. It would take them two or three days to get there depending on the route and speed they traveled. Ricky had said we wasn't allowed to speed so going by that we could figure it a little closer. The car was the one I had seen at the movies that night. Arkie and the chief said they were going to call some friends and get some help for surveillance for them along the way. The chief put that big ham of a hand on my shoulder and said, "take it easy Thomas were not going to let anything happen to her. " I knew it was his way of saying things were Ok between us.

I said, " thanks chief and ran to the bathroom and puked." The beer and the pain pill finally gave way and went down the drain together. I felt better but weak. Arkie came out of the chiefs office smiling. Got a hold of an old army pal Buddy Owens he,s on the force in New Orleans now. Chief said and Lt. Eddy of the state patrol will keep the roads clear in Arizona, Capt. Jones in New Mexico, Capt. Wright in Texas and Lt. Somers in Louisiana so we got that covered. Now we just need to wait. I jumped up from my desk. I should have taken it easy I got weak again. You can wait but I'm going to New Orleans, Arkie said me too. The chief shrugged his shoulders and handed me his city credit card. Use it easy he said, and keep in touch at least twice a day.

We went back to Crystals house and got more new clothes. Hell might as well use them, if things go wrong no one else will need them. I stood there in the driveway, just looking around. Arkie said, "whats bothering you hoss?" I said Ok we know Ricky killed the girls, did the hair and Jonathon told him to do the notes. We know Mrs. Adams drugged me. We know Crystal and Ricky are related, step brother and sister. Jonathon got a thing for Crystal. Were not sure who killed the girl in New York, my bet is on Jonathon. We know Crystal was either kidnapped or went voluntary with Ricky to New Orleans, my bet is on kidnapped. "So" he said. Well we don't know who shot me. I need to know that. I'm still hurting and we don't even have a suspect. He said, were working on it hoss. Mayo got some ideas. As we left on the way to the airport I said, "could it have been Crystal." He shrugged his shoulders. What do you think hoss? No it couldn't have been her I hear her rush out of the house when she came to me. I remember hearing the door slam. And where would she have put the gun. It hasn't been found yet. Again more questions than answers. And what is Mayo working on about my shooting? Are they keeping something from me, if so why? Somehow no matter what the evidence says I still feel this all somehow goes back to Alex Zapata.

I called Shaw to the side and ask him to check up on Zapata without the chief knowing about it. He smiled no problem but why. I shrugged just a feeling. He nodded. I'll have something by the time you get back from New Orleans if not sooner. On the way to the airport Arkie was on his cell phone calling his friend in New Orleans to pick us up. I ask him again about Mayo. Don't sweat it hoss, were all working for you. I just couldn't get it out of my mind I was being passed up on something important. The plane was full and we had to bump two people from the flight. They were students going back to Tulane. We slipped them a few bucks extra for their seats although we didn't have to. Good public relations.

The flight was good and quick. Buddy met us at the airport. Arkie and Buddy could have been brothers. Both were about the same size, same beer belly, same almost bald, and both had that swagger. He took us to Chilis for dinner saying he wanted to show off his latest conquest. She was another Rose, over forty, with big boob and tried to act sexy. Plus she was trying to do the wife bit, did you take your blood pressure medicine. I swear he would forget it if I didn't keep after him about it. He ordered for all us. Once you taste the chicken here Col. Sanders will be a thing in the past. They set talking about old times. The billboard across the street grabbed my attention.

Arkie said something to me I guess. I didn't answer . He said it again and shook me. Hoss what's wrong with you? I said look at the billboard across the street. Remind you of anyone you know. It was a girl in a very sexy pose. The reading said, "Jade the real jewel of Bourbon Street appearing nightly at Mamas Bar. He said, " shit she looks just like Crystal. When he turned to Buddy. Do you know her? No been here about a month or two, looker ain,t she?

Arkis told him she looked just like Crystal our mayor who was kidnapped and was on her way here now with Ricky Adams. He said we can go see her tonight, Arkie agreed. I told them I was still hurting and was staying in. Need to check with the chief anyway. He said he had just talked to Big Red as he called the chief right before he picked us up. I ask if the surveillance of them was going Ok. He laughed boy I could tell you what color their underwear is if you want to know. I'm good at my job. I told him I didn't doubt it, I was just antsy. Arkie said, "the mayor is also Thomas real love. He nodded. Shes ok. You just rest tonight. Me and Arkie going out. He can see if Jade really looks like your mayor or if its all makeup. He had checked us in to The Orleans Motor Lodge, it was as close to the Sheridan as we could get. He told us he had friends at the Sheridan who would keep him advised about Jonathon's coming and goings. Well he did have to wait at least two days hard driving for Ricky and Crystal to get there, and Jonathon had told Ricky to take it easy so all we could do is wait.

Arkie wanted to see the night life of New Orleans OK with me. I knew he would be there when I needed him. Buddy picked him up about 7, he said, " you sure its Ok hoss?" Sure go ahead if I'm not here when you get back, I'm at the bar. They left. I laid down to rest, still not 100% yet. I tossed and turned, watched TV, just couldn't get rested so fuck it I got up. I decided to walk down to Mamas Bar to look around. It wasn't too far away maybe 3 blocks or so.

There were street hustlers every few steps I just ignored them. The bar wasn't much. When I enter I realized it was a gay bar or close to it. Mama was a 300lbs. drag queen. He sided up to me and smiled. His breath smelled of stale cigarettes and cheap wine. You new here honey? Just passing through, though I'd look around. Heard there was a real cutie here named Jade. His face screwed up. Left yesterday not even with so much as a kiss my ass. But I've got others here, want someone, male or female up to you I swing both ways myself. Interested? I shook my head. He signaled the barman over. This is my new friend, Whats your name anyway? Called me Jesse, you know like Jesse James. He laughed that smell again. Well Jesse this drinks on me. Stay around I think we could be friends.

I picked up the beer and sort of floated toward the back of the bar out of sight to look things over, good thing I did. In about 5 minutes Jonathon came In dressed in skin tight purple pants with a green tee shirt that showed off his muscles. Yeah he had spent some time in the gym. He was also wearing cowboy boots, that pissed me off. Mama seemed to know him they kissed on the lips, yuck. Mama called someone or something over Jonathon also kissed it. In a minute they left together.

I left by the back door. I didn't want anyone to see me there especially Jonathon. Arkie and Buddy still weren't home, home is where ever I happen to be. They stumbled in a couple hours later, both drunk out of their minds. Id never seen Arkie so drunk, made me wonder what he had been drinking. He fell on the bed and passed out. Buddy said, "see you in the morning and stumbled out the door." I lay there awake thinking about Crystal and Jade, Ricky, Richard and Mrs. Adams aka Mrs. Read, Mrs. Zapata just wondering how they were all involved and Jonathon. I was sure he was gay so what was his interest in Crystal when they worked together. And if Crystal and Jade looked so much alike were they just sisters or maybe twins. Mrs. Read Crystals mother must have known. If they were twins would she just give one of them up.

I called the chief out of bed. He wasn't too happy about it. I told him about my suspicions. He said he would look into it in the morning, now if I didn't mind he was going back to sleep. He sort of slammed the phone down. Finally I passed out too. The phone woke me, it was Buddy wanting to speak to Arkie. He got on the phone still smelling of last night. He said hello then just listened. Said thanks and hung up. The staff at Sheridan told Buddy Jade was there in Jonathons room. The thing he picked up last night only stayed an hour. When it left its face was bleeding very badly. They offered to call the cops or take it to the hospital. It ran out the door shaking its head no.

I told Arkie about my going to Mamas Bar last night and seeing Jonathon picking it up. I ask about Jade the owner said she had just disappeared with out a kiss my ass or anything. Arkie said what now? Now we get breakfast after you shower and brush your teeth. I've never seen you so drunk. Yeah Buddy took me to a voo doo place last night. They passed the drink around, I drank some. Powerful stuff. I called the chief again while he showered. He still wasn't too happy to hear from me. I just got in, but I've got Van Buren, and Mayo working on it. A lot of those old records before we got everything on computer are gone, lost. He slammed the phone down again. Big deal. I know I'm on to something just don't know what, yet.

We went to breakfast at Cajon Kitchen right across the street from the Sheridan. I thought if we happen to see Jonathon or Jade I would say we were in town on police business, maybe get him to thinking. Buddy joined us in a few minutes. Arkie had called him while I showered and told him where we were going for breakfast. Said we should have gone to Chilis, great breakfast there too plus he could see his baby. They started bullshitting again, I turned them out. I was still very worried about Crystal they acted as if nothing was happening. Plus I was watching for Jonathon and Jade. We took a couple hours for breakfast, mostly just drinking coffee and watching. Finally we took the hint by the waiter and left.

I ask Buddy about the serveance as they were traveling. He said no sweat its being handled. Shit man I could ever tell you what they had for breakfast, just take it easy. I nodded .Easy for him to say he didn't have the interest in the case I have. If things go according to plan they should arrive in New Orleans between 2 and 4 tomorrow afternoon. We spent some of the day just looking around. I'd been there before but tried to act as normal as possible to all we were seeing. Yes New Orleans is an exciting place but my heart just wasn't in it. Of course we had to go to Chilis again for dinner so Buddy could see his squeeze.

Again I noticed the billboard but didn't say anything about it instead I suggest to go over to Hooters to get a beer. Arkie was all for it but Buddy was afraid his girlfriend would see us. It was visible from Chilis just almost below the Jade billboard. Their not ever married and he is already 'whipped" know what I mean? Arkie decided to stay in tonight and rest he knew tomorrow could be heavy. We sat and watched wrestling for a while. He went out and got some beers, we drank them then turned in. I was sort of dozing. It was getting close to midnight when the phone rang, it was the chief. Did I wake you and he laughed. Mayo found the birth certificate for Crystal. Yes Jade was her twin. There are no other paper work about them. Either Mrs. Read just gave her away or something else happened we don't know about. No records of her going to school here or actually anywhere in the U.S. we could find.

Don't worry Thomas well get it all straightened out after you get the S.O.B. tomorrow. Did you remember the election is tomorrow. I'm afraid Crystal might lose because of this shit. Well Thomas keep me advised tomorrow and you and Arkie be careful. You know that S.O.B. has killed at least 4 we know about. I said we would and thanked him for the info. I hung up.

But of course I couldn't get back to sleep. I lay there thrashing around for hours listening to Arkie snore until at last the sleep God carried me home. I woke up late, Arkie was setting in his underwear drinking coffee. A beautiful sight on waking. He handed me a cup. He said, New Orleans style got something else in it. Not my taste but I drank it anyway. We got dressed and went to breakfast, Buddy met us there again. So much was suppose to happen today, my stomach was jittery. I pushed my pancakes around the plate, Arkie and Buddy ate like horses. Buddys phone went off. After he answered it his face got very red and shouted ,"you fuckin idiots." He stood there fuming. Sorry Thomas but they got away from us. We don't know where they are.

They checked into the Paris Motel in Orange Texas. The survelius team got a room too. Taking turns staying awake in case they left in the night. This morning after 10 they went to the office to check on them even thought their car was still there. The manager had the cleaning lady go say "room service: no one answered. She opened the door they were gone. Clean as a whistle. Most have left by the back way.

Well keep the team watching the motel here. Jonathon has also checked out of the Sheridan along with Jade theirs all gone sorry.

Sorry! I shouted you are a bunch of fuckin stupid assholes. The dumbest cop in Phoenix knows better than you bunch of fuck ups. I balled up my fist. I was ready to kick his ass. Arkie grabbed my arms. Who hoss. They fucked up, we done it before. Set down well figure it out.

My phone went off, it was the chief. He told me about the same thing Buddy had just said. He said come home, nothing you can do there. They are all probably in Mexico by now. By the way the poles close in two hours Crystal is winning so far. He hung up. I didn't care if she was winning or not ,what good would that do if she was dead with an ice pick stuck in her brain. So we went back to Phoenix after Arkie told Buddy thanks for the help. Buddy came to me and just said sorry. He stuck out his hand I didn't shake his hand I was too pissed.

The chief and Mayo met us at the airport. There wasn't much said on the way to the squad. All the other detectives came over and told me don't worry we'll get this bastard and Crystal will be Ok. I know they meant well but it didn't help any. I just went home. The place looked lonely but clean. I wandered around the house drinking beer. The phone rang several times I didn't answer it. I got really drunk that night and slept in till almost noon the next day. Someone coming in the front door wakened me. It was Marie. She said sorry Tomas I didn't know for sure if you was home. I see your car outside sorry again.

I said no sweat I'm late for work see you later. I got dressed with out showering, brushing my teeth or shaving I must have really smelt. I got in the car. I honked the horn. Marie came out of the house. I said how much do I owe you? She just said later ok? I waved and drove away. No one even looked up as I entered the squad. The chief called me in his office. He said set down and listen don't talk. I sat. Thomas we all know how this has effected you. I started to speak. He held up his hand for silence. Just listen. You are going on vacation for two weeks. I have a place in Sonora. Go stay there we will get this asshole and we will get Crystal back. You are too involved in this. I don't blame you but you have been known to go off half cocked. We are afraid you might do something stupid. We don't want you to do something that some smart ass lawyer can use and get the SOB off. Now get the hell out of here before I kick your ass.

He handed me the keys and address to his place in Sonora. Arkie came over to me, don't sweat it hoss, I'll keep in touch. You can use the rest. I noticed several times you are still hurting from being shot. Take care, he hugged me and left very quickly.

I peeled out of the parking lot and headed south. I hit the freeway on the way to Nogales. I entered Mexico and checked in the first motel I could find. There wasn't even sheets on the bed. It was a dirty flop house but I didn't care. I just wanted to drink till all the pain went away. I got a case of Coronas brought to my room. I drank till I passed out. I woke up sometime in the night. Through the paper thin walls I could hear a baby cry somewhere down the hall. I got up from the smelly pee stained bare mattress and went to the roach invested john. Did natures call. I popped a Marlboro, crumbled the pack down to my last smoke again. I stood at the window nude watching the neon light streak the sky. I pulled on a pair of jeans and a tee shirt. Stumbled downstairs to the cantina below. Ate some tacos with some kind of meat, cat maybe. Bought more beers and went back to the room. Thats all I did for 3 or 4 days I'm not sure really how long I was there. I didn't bath, brush my teeth nothing. I just wanted the pain to go away. When I was drunk I didn't feel the hurt.

A banging on the door finally brought me out of my drunken slumber. It was Arkie. He threw me in the shower, the ice cold water brought me around. I threw up till there was nothing left, then I got the dry heaves. I sat there on the edge of that dirty mattress shaking. Arkie brought me some food and a big pot of coffee. He forced me to eat and drink all the coffee. I stopped once to throw up, he made me continue. He dragged me out of there and took me to the Big 8 Motel a few miles away close to the border. He made me stay in the car as he registered us in. They see you no way would we get a room. He hustled me back into the shower and handed me a bar of soap and shampoo. I felt very weak but managed to get it all done. I looked in the mirror. I looked like hell. Arkie had put a razor on the counter, I scrapped off what I could. I cut myself a few times. The beard was longer than I thought it should have been. My hair was also longer. Arkis said," chief got worried when we didn't hear from you after a week, so I came looking."

A week, how long have I been here? Ten days or so. Ten days Shit? We arent sure if you came right here or stopped someway along the way. He had brought me clothes to wear from my house. The jeans were a little loose, so was the shirt but the boots still fit. We went across the street to KFC, I ate like I hadn't in a week, maybe I hadn't. This time Arkie paid. He said the chief had given him money. Ok Thomas this is whats happening on the case. At a bar in Nogales called Mamas Bar, "name sound familiar" there is a dancer called Jade. I think it's the same one from New Orleans, Crystals sister. Tonight we go there and check it out.

As far as Crystal we havent heard anything from either her or Ricky. Jonathon we traced to the London. Hes still there doing the gay bar tour. We took most of the day just going on what we really knew, it wasn't too much. The part that bothered me was what happened to Crystals father in Mexico. How did he get involved with Alex Zapata and Eve Zapata AKA Else Adams her two sons were they his real or adopted children and how did Jonathon fit in. He was an educated lawyer although a gay not a bottom feeder like the others. The information was here in Mexico, not really in our jurisdiction. But right then I didn't give a shit. I spent most of the day laying around resting and eating. I only drank 1 beer and I couldn't finish it. I'd lost my taste for it I guess. Arkie finished the rest of the 6 pack.

As it was getting dark we wandered down to the bar section of Nogales. Mamas Bar was on the bottom part of the strip. We walked in. It even looked like the one in New Orleans except all the customers but us were Mexicans. Dark with a bunch of perverts hanging around, some in drag. You ever see a fat Mexican stuffed into a mini skirt with a hairy chest. Not a pretty sight. Someone or something sort of floated up to us. It grinned, not too many teeth and what was left were rotten and black. The smell almost gagged me. Hey Gringo you want boy or girl or maybe me. It grinned again. I said I want Jade. He started cussing, everyone wants Jade fucking Puta. You too early Jade comes maybe 11 O, Clock. I nodded. It laughed again but she come many times tonight. You want Jade better you wait with me.

Arkie grabbed my arm. We'll come back later. We backed out the door. He grabbed my arm, that one in the mini skirt rubbed my ass made me almost puke. I said I know the feeling. We went across the street to another cantina. This one with outdoor tables. We got a couple of Coronos and waited. I said, " you know Arkie everyone Says Jade is the image of Crystal, why would someone that looks like that have anything to do with that scum?" He shook his head. I don't know hoss I wondered that myself.

His phone went off, it was the chief. He just listened then hung up. Well heres another bit of news. Crystals father was a science teacher. Chiefs friends in the Feds say he was involved with Zapata in the drug business.The boys may have been Zapatas or Reads no way to find out now. And Mrs. Adams is Zapata real sister. So anyway you look at it this is a screwed up family. Chief said he was close in case we needed him. We saw a few underage kids from Arizona drinking and smoking weed. Easy enough to do in Mexico.

A limo pulled up in front of Mamas Bar. Several gun toting men got out, then the star Jade. She took my breath away for a second, yes she looked and moved like Crystal. Then an old man got out could it possibly be Crystal father Mr. Charles Read in person. It was hard to tell his age from where we sat but he was old. Walked slowly and sort of bent over. Jade took his arm and they enter the bar. We sat there a few more minutes till it looked like Mamas Bar was closing. We ran across the street. Mini skirt was closing the front door. O its you gringo come in we close when Jade come. Show time now.

The crowd was grouped around a small stage in the back of the bar. The old man sat on a high stool at its side. The stage was bathed in a soft pink spotlight. Several people went to the old man and gave him money. He smiled, clean white straight teeth, maybe dentures. Music started, it was low and sexy. Jade came out on stage dressed in a white wedding gown. She slowly stripped, it was strangely sexy. When she got down to her G string she turned her back When she turned around I almost lost all of my KFC. There between her legs hung a PENIS. A real one not a snap on. Id hear about that before. They called it chicks with dicks. She certainly was a girl with something extra. It was unsettling to be sure.

Then from the rear of the stage entered Ricky Adams. They kissed and started having sex right there in front of everyone. The crowd had shoved us to the front of the stage. Ricky raised his head from his sexual activity and saw me. He smirked and winked at me. I wanted to climb up there and kick his ass, but we were in a foreign country and had no official business there. Arlie grabbed my arm, he knew what I was thinking. He shook his head no said not now.

The people who had given the old man money joined in the activity on stage. We started toward the door. Mini skirt stopped us. No one leaves till the show is over. Why don't you join in? I was really getting sick then.

A loud whistle blew and the door was knocked off its hinges. A load of cops some in swat wear entered throwing people against the walls and on the floor. They shoved us aside. I looked toward the stage both Jade and the old man were gone. Ricky had also disappeared into the shadows. The chief was there along with Lt. Migual Sanches head of the feds in Mexico. He rounded up all the people there most were fugitives from the law one way or the other. Their called bajadores or common criminals. One cop came in and whispered something in Lt. Sanches ear. He smiled and turned to the chief. I have a present for you. Because you cant take him in custody in Mexico he will be waiting in a van right across the border handcuffed to a chair. Here is the key. Chief motioned to Arkie take him to Phoenix. Thomas you wait here with me. We got somewhere else to go. The feds took the others away.

We got in a jeep with the Lt. plus two more cop. The chief and I sat in back the others squeezed in front. We drove for a couple of hours on dusty bumpy roads into the countryside. There was no moon it was very dark. We enter a small compound. It was made in a circular style. It had 3 or 4 shacks. A light shone from one in the back. We all jumped out of the jeep. The two officers enter first. We waited outside. One motioned us in. There on the bed stripped nude was Crystal.

She was duck taped to the bed. Her lays spread wide apart. A gag in her mouth. Blood was all over her, it was still running slowly down her legs. She was trying to get away from us. The tape cutting into her flesh. I took the gag from her mouth. She screamed. I said, " its ok honey its me Thomas." She continued screaming shoving me away. Lt. Sanches took out a needle and shoved it into her leg. She shook a few times then went limp.

We noticed a tape machine in the corner. We turned it on. There was Jade raping Crystal. I threw up. Can you picture that in your mind. The same face, hair breast but below the waist very different. The look on Crystals face was of sheer fear. Jade looked like she was having a great time. Then others were having sex with Crystal. I went outside and threw up again.

Chief said Thomas we got to get Crystal back to Phoenix and in the hospital NOW. That shot will keep her out about 3 hours. I ask how about the border. Its being taking care of he said. I knew what that meant. We bundled her in the jeep using the blankets from her bed still soaked in blood. I swear to God I'm going to make someone pay for this. The driver took a shorter route back just as dusty and bumpy but shorter.

We transfer Crystal into a police car. The Lt. drove us through the border. He got out. He said something to the chief, to me he said bastard will pay. He shook my hand and left. The chief got behind the wheel. I never saw him drive so fast. We pulled up at 24th street in 1 hour 40 minutes. Now some of you may know 24 and Van Buren is the State Hospital for the Insane. Chief said better we hide her here till we know all that's happened. I've arranged for total privacy. Thomas he shook my shoulder snap out of it. This is the best thing for now. They brought out a stretcher I wouldnt let them us it. I carried her in. Then the doctors took over. They tried to shoo us out but I wouldnt leave. This was the woman I wanted to be the mother of my children. I wasn't going anywhere. They just worked around me. They washed off the surface blood. She was still bleeding between her legs and bruises covered most of her body. I hadn't noticed them before I was so caught up in all the blood. The doc said we must do surgery right away or she will die.

The chief gave his Ok, and signed the permission form. They finally got me pushed away and took her in for surgery. We sat outside waiting just waiting. I prayed a lot then silently. I'm sure the chief did too. They were in surgery 6 hours or more. Arkie came sometime while it was going on. He talked to the chief saying he had to restrain Ricky along the way. Not too bad I broke his nose and a couple of ribs, but there is enough left to put on trial. But there wasn't, sometime during the night someone slit his throat. Too bad I wanted to see the asshole die in old sparkie.

Crystal never returned to normal and now lives full time at 24 th Street. She still screams whenever anyone touches her. For months afterward I went ever week to see her until the doc said don't come any more. It upsets her. James Nelson took over for mayor by proxie. Mrs. Adams pleaded guilty and was given life in prison without possible of parole. At the trial she finally admitted she was the one who had shot me saying if Id killed you they would have never solved this case and my boy would still be alive. Then she tried to spit on me. The killing in New York was probably done by Jonathon none of our business anyway.

He has moved to Brazil where we have no extration Arkie moved in with Rose I think it lasted 6 months or so.It took a while but I finally got all the information I wanted. This is the way it happened as far as I can find out. After Charles Read took Jade and went to Mexico. He needed someone to watch her while he worked in the drug business with Zapata. At the time Eve Zapata was young, sexy and available. So they all lived together in a house. When Eve got pregnant it wasn't sure who the father was because she was having sex both with her brother Zapata and Charles Read. To them it didn't seem to matter. Jade was raised as a girl, but a girl with a secret. After a while Mr. Read dropped by the wayside sexually but kept in touch with Zapata and Eve. The boys were raised as if they were one. After Zapata was jailed in Phoenix and sent to prison. It was somewhere in this time she married and killed Max Adams after she hade changed her name and those of the boys to Adams .Eve came to Arizona and worked as a housekeeper with the ex mayor. Crystal just let her keep the job. Zapatas were very happy Crystal was now mayor. They knew who she was but she didn't know about them. I couldn't find out what happened to Jade. Mr. Read was found in a motel in El Paso dead, the police said of a heart attack. After a while I finally went back to work just me and Arkie again, against the world.

Most nights now I set on the porch at home thinking about what might have been. There is an old Willie Nelson song that goes. They tell me in time I'll forget about you, but somehow I cant find the time.

THE END

About the Author

Denzil Casto has worked in several countries around the world such as the Philippines, Thailand, and Somali. He has completed another book about an orphan raised by the Mafia. He is currently working on another "Thomas Thomas" thriller, again based on a true event.